This book belongs to

....

....

Contents

We Wish You A Merry Christmas

p

We Wish You a Merry Christmas!

We wish you a merry Christmas!
We wish you a merry Christmas!
We wish you a merry Christmas
And a happy New Year!
Glad tidings we bring
To you and your kin.
We wish you a merry Christmas
And a happy New Year!

Snowman

With coal-black eyes and carrot nose,
I have no fingers, legs, or toes.
My skin is icy cold to touch,
Yet you don't see me wearing much!
A woolly scarf, a battered hat–
I'm lucky if I'm dressed in that!
I can't lift my arms, run round, or bend,
But I make a wonderful playtime friend.
I'm only around for a while each year,
And you never know when I'll disappear!

A Present for Santa

Rachel sat at the kitchen table, clicking her knitting needles.

"What are you making?" asked Mum.

"A present," replied Rachel.

"Is it for Dad?" asked Mum.

"No," laughed Rachel. "Guess again."

"Tom?" said Mum. Tom was Rachel's brother. Rachel shook her head. "Well, maybe Granny, then?"

But Rachel just grinned. "It's a surprise," she said. "You'll have to wait!"

In the week before Christmas, the red strip of knitting grew longer and longer. Rachel sat knitting whenever she could.

"I know what it is," said Mum. "It's a scarf!" Rachel nodded.

"But who is it for?" asked Mum and started to guess again. She tried all the people she could think of – Grandpa, Uncle Philip – even the dog! But she was wrong every time!"

"You'll have to wait and see," Rachel said, smiling.

So, Mum went on decorating the Christmas tree and Rachel continued with her knitting.

By Christmas Eve, the scarf was finished. Rachel wrapped it up and tied a big, red ribbon around it. Then she wrote a label, stuck it on the parcel and put it by the fireplace.

"Aren't you going to put it under the Christmas tree?" asked Mum.

"No," said Rachel, shaking her head, firmly.

"Ah," said Mum. "Now I think I know who it's for."

On Christmas morning, Rachel found a note by the fireplace, where the present had been. It read:

Dear Rachel,
Thank you for the beautiful scarf. Just the thing to keep me warm on my sleigh.
        Love Father Christmas.

        xxx

Santa's Little Helpers

Santa's little helpers
Are getting in a tizzy.
It's very nearly Christmas,
And the workshop's really busy!
There's a great, big stack of letters
Still sitting on the shelf.
"We're never going to make it!"
Says a worried little elf.
"There's piles of presents left to wrap,
And all these bows to tie.
The bicycles have got no bells.
I think I'm going to cry!"

13

"Come on, you must work faster!"
Shouts old Bert, the elf in charge.
"Put pink tags on the little gifts
And purple on the large."
So then, the elves all dash and rush,
With hammers, paint and glue.
"You've painted that car red!" yells Bert.
"You know it should be blue!"
The clock strikes twelve, the elves all sigh,
At last, the work is done.
They wave good-bye to Santa,
And now it's time for fun!

14

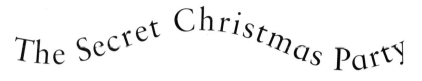

The Secret Christmas Party

One snowy Christmas Eve, down on Thistlewood Farm,
Jo, Tom and Ellie sneaked out of their beds
and ran across the farmyard to the big barn.

Their daddy had promised them that, on the
stroke of midnight, all the animals would begin
to talk! Could it be true? They just had to find
out. So, very carefully, they pushed open the
wooden barn door and crept inside.

All the animals were snuggled up
cosily in the straw.

"When are they going to talk?"
whispered little Ellie, yawning.

Ellie's big brother, Tom, looked at his watch.
"Right... now!" he cried.

But there wasn't a sound!

"Perhaps they're shy," suggested Jo. "Let's hide."
So Tom, Jo and Ellie hid behind an old cart and waited... and
waited... and waited!

Finally, the children peeped over the top.
The animals were peeping back – and still not talking!

"It isn't true," moaned Ellie. "It's just one of Dad's stories.
Let's go back to bed."

Sadly, the children trudged back home. But, back in the barn...

"Yippee!" shouted Tod the Horse. "I thought they'd never go."
And all the animals began to laugh and chatter!

"Come on," boomed Bertie the Bull. "Let's party!" The hens
made sandwiches and the cows gave jugs of warm, frothy milk.
What a wonderful feast!

After they had finished eating, the ducks sang noisily and
everyone started dancing.

Tod waltzed Dolly the Donkey around the barn, and they all did the Hokey-Cokey. Tilly the Cow won Hunt the Horseshoe and Gus the Goat was great at Blind Goat's Bluff.

"Right," laughed Bertie. "Everyone outside for a snowball fight!"

"Hurray!" cheered the animals, tumbling out into the farmyard and hurling fat, fluffy snowballs at each other.

What fun they had, slipping and sliding about!

Up in the farmhouse, little Ellie was fast asleep, but Tom and Jo were wide awake.

"I wish it were true," murmured Jo with a sigh. "I wish the animals could talk on Christmas Eve."

"So do I," replied Tom sleepily. "But it's only a story, just like Father Christmas."

Down in the farmyard, the animals kept on playing and, up on the roof, Father Christmas smiled!